How God Got Christian
Into Trouble

By the same author
Shadow of a Bull (1965 Newbery Award winner)
Odyssey of Courage:
   The Story of Cabeza de Vaca
A Kingdom in a Horse
The Hollywood Kid
A Single Light
Tuned Out
"Hey, What's Wrong with This One?"
The Rotten Years
Don't Play Dead Before You Have To
The Life and Death of a Brave Bull
Through the Broken Mirror with Alice
Till the Break of Day

Under the name of Maia Rodman, a novel for adults
The People in His Life

How God Got Christian Into Trouble

by
Maia Wojciechowska

Illustrated by
Les Gray

WP

THE WESTMINSTER PRESS
Philadelphia

Book design by Christine Schueler

First edition

Published by The Westminster Press®
Philadelphia, Pennsylvania

PRINTED IN THE UNITED STATES OF AMERICA
2 4 6 8 9 7 5 3 1

Library of Congress Cataloging in Publication Data

Wojciechowska, Maia, 1927–
How God got Christian into trouble.

SUMMARY: God assumes the form of a young child and
spends a few days with eleven-year-old Christian Wolny in
New York, meeting his family and friends, going to church
and school, talking about life, death, and love, and
affecting people's lives in various ways.
1. Children's stories, American. [1. God—Fiction]
I. Gray, Leslie, ill. II. Title.
PZ7.W8183Ho 1984   [Fic]   84-15381
ISBN 0-664-32717-6

for Leonora

Whether your faith is that there is a God or that there is not a God, if you don't have any doubts you are either kidding yourself or asleep.
God cannot be expressed but only experienced.

Frederick Buechner
Wishful Thinking: A Theological ABC

"But as God, you have the power to intervene, to help us in emergencies."

"So when do I draw the line? Say a fella is going to eat a hamburger that's not one-hundred-percent beef. What do I do, knock it out of his hands? How would you like to live with Divine Hands popping out of the sky all the time? It would make people crazy."

Avery Corman
Oh, God!

THE BEST thing, I guess, would be to start at the beginning. And that would have to be last Tuesday when I got Grandpa's letter. Things were pretty messed up over at my house for some time. For one thing my father had been living in the guest room for the past few months. He moved there when Mom began training the ladies of WOW (Women of the World) for their assault on the White House rose garden. That's when he moved to the guest room and took my Magic Markers with him and made a banner out of a sheet. The banner is hanging out of the guest-room window, and if you look up as you round 84th and Park, you can see it in the air shaft. What he wrote on the sheet is this: MEN, THEY'RE AFTER US.

I worry about my parents a lot, and I worry about almost everything and everyone else as well. I even got an ulcer, which is something else that worries me because my doctor, David Perkel, is writing an article about it for some medical journal and he's also mentioning the fact that I'm losing my hair prematurely. If that article ever comes out, I'll probably feel like a real freak, which is something else to worry about.

Anyway, the letter from my grandfather came on Tuesday. It was postmarked from the Vatican because that's where he's been living for the past ten years. It said:

Dear Christian,
You will receive this letter only if I'm dead, because I promised your father that I will not tell you anything while I'm alive. Over the years your father and I used to have many arguments about who is going to tell you about your proud heritage. Your father happens to think our heritage "un-American" and "unhealthy." The way he wanted it, nobody would ever tell you about it, and that is not right, because knowledge is always preferable to ignorance. So I'm doing it from beyond the grave, so to speak. I've made arrangements to have this letter sent to you upon my death.

Ever since Poland became a Christian nation, back in the ninth century, every second generation of males in the Wolny family has heard voices. The voices were of martyrs, of saintly widows and virgins, of men and women who lived and died for their faith. Those voices were heard over the centuries by your male ancestors. Some of them were imprisoned, most were ridiculed, a few committed to insane asylums, and one or two even put to death, and all because they were chosen, I suppose by God, to hear voices. I was fifteen myself when I first heard St. Christopher's voice. St. Chris has been wonderful company to me over all these years. Anyway, I am going to meet him personally, in heaven. Even if he's not a saint, I know he's there.

10

Consider yourself lucky, Christian. Your life, when you begin to hear a voice of your own, might become more difficult, but it will be much more exciting in every way. Some people, including your parents and your friends, may think you're nuts and may even try to "cure" you. And I bet you'll get into trouble. But no matter what happens, you'll be carrying on a grand old tradition. Don't you ever feel ashamed of being a Wolny. Yours is a very rare, a very precious inherited gift. So be of good cheer.

Your loving grandfather

There was also a P.S. It said:

A few of the Wolnys, it seems, got boring voices. Should you get a boring one, don't be discouraged. All our ancestors with boring voices went deaf early in life.

The crummy thing was that, when I was reading Grandpa's letter, I didn't even think of him as being dead. All I could think about was getting some insane voice inside my head. And that's all I needed. I mean, I was going bananas already.

That first day I thought I could forget all about it, or maybe that I wouldn't even get a voice, living in New York City and all. I mean, my ancestors lived in Poland, and their voices probably talked to them in Polish, and I don't even know the language! And besides, maybe in America it's unconstitutional to hear voices. . . .

11

*   *   *

Well, nothing really unusual happened from Tuesday, when I got that letter, to my last class on Friday, which is Miss Rosetta Ball's English composition class. She's not really a teacher, you see, but a writer: the author of that best-seller, *I Was a Man for a Week.* Now she's pretending to be a teacher. I'm the only person—besides the principal, that is—who knows she's really Esther Schwartstein instead of Miss Rosetta Ball. The reason I know is because she picked me up once in a taxi. It was raining like crazy, and she spotted me in the rain and gave me a ride to school. She told me that she's got this big contract to write this book about being a teacher in a public school. I just know it's going to be lousy because she's such a phony. Anyway, the first time I heard the voice was in her class.

The voice said, "Christian, why do you worry so?"

That's what the voice asked. I didn't know where to look, because the voice didn't come from any special place. It was just there. Nobody else seemed to have heard it. Everyone was listening to Freddy Wallace read his composition. Just before I heard the voice, I was worried about that—Freddy's composition, I mean. He had copied it right out of a book I'd loaned him.

I was also worried about how nobody knows what a real jerk that Freddy Wallace is. He's an A student, but he's always cheating and never gets caught. I was also worrying that maybe one day Freddy Wallace would become President of the United States. I

12

mean, he's our class president, and all the teachers
think he's the neatest kid, and all the parents who go
to PTA meetings are always coming up to Mr. and
Mrs. Wallace, telling them what a great example
their son is to everybody. Freddy Wallace is the
school blackmailer, and everyone's scared of him. He
beats up on kids and then makes them say what a
great guy he is.

I was also worried that the bell might not ring
before I was called to read my composition, which
was real awful. Anyway, right after Freddy Wallace
had read the stuff he stole, Miss Rosetta Ball gives us
all this meaningful look and says, "Now that's what I
call a good composition." Miss Ball is all wired up,
and everything she says, or anyone says, gets taped,
and all that stuff is typed up by her secretary each
night. I hope she edits out everything I ever said. But
I just knew my dumb composition was going to end
up among all those notes and stuff for her lousy book.

"All right, Christian Wolny, let's hear what you
did."

Did I ever hate reading my dumb composition that
day! Philomena Garcia didn't make it any easier, either. She sits right in front of me, and she's got this
crazy habit of always turning around and putting
her chin in both her hands and staring at me
each time I stand up, and often she does it even
when I don't. I once passed this note saying it
bothers me, her staring at me, and she passed me
one saying that she adores staring "adoringly" at me.
The worst thing is that she goes around saying she's

going to marry me one day!

Anyway, my lousy composition went something like this:

What American Indians Mean to Me

The whole thing about Indians worries me a lot. The old Westerns, from which I got all my ideas about them, taught me that they were bad guys always killing women and children. The good guys, like the Duke, John Wayne, that is, had to go out and kill them. Now, if all that is no longer true, where does it leave the Duke? And me?

I was never personally acquainted with any Indians. I saw some, once, when we went to Santa Fe, New Mexico. They were selling junk on the plaza, but it was all too expensive and cheap looking, and when I said that to a couple of Indian ladies, they said a bad word to me and told me to scram. I really don't know what to say about Indians, since I don't know the truth about them. I suppose if they were the native Americans, those who came to visit didn't act much like guests. But all I know is this, if I were an Indian I would either want to belong to this country or else be represented at the United Nations, as a nation or something. I suppose we've learned a lot of lies about Indians, but I am not sure that what we are being told today is much better. It seems to me like a bunch of half lies, so I can't say they mean much to me. Sorry about that.

Just as I finished reading this lousy composition, I heard the voice for the second time.

"I like your composition, Christian. It's honest, and I like honesty very much."

I couldn't even get too excited about the voice saying that to me, because Philomena Garcia pats my left hand with her right, and Miss Rosetta Ball says, "I don't know that you worked your behind off on that one. The way I feel is that the Indians should get the Southwest and the blacks should get Africa."

That starts a row among the Puerto Ricans, who want Manhattan, and then some black kids start shouting that they didn't want Africa and they'd take California instead. And then the bell rang, and there was the usual rush for the door.

Right after that, old Philomena comes rushing at me. A few of her girlfriends are right behind her. And while she's talking to me—yelling at me, really —she keeps looking back at her friends.

"Hey, my mom says it would be O.K. for you to take me to a movie."

I figure she must have begged her mother for months for permission, and though it makes me sick even to think about being with her in the dark, I don't want to hurt her feelings, especially in front of her girlfriends, who are all waiting to see what I'll say to her.

"Let's do that someday," I say. "Let's take in a movie."

"If you don't have any money," Philomena Garcia

says, "that's all right. I'll pay. I've saved over twenty dollars from baby-sitting."

"If I take you, I'll pay," I say, and her girlfriends all applaud.

"Will you take me Saturday?"

"Maybe in a couple of weeks," I say, and she looks very happy and skips away. I know I lied to her and lying worries me, but just then I hear the voice, for the third time.

"By next week," the voice says, "she'll forget you even exist. By then she'll be madly in love with Steve Parker."

That was when I talked back to the voice for the first time.

"How do you know?" I asked.

"I know everything," the voice says. "That's part of my business. Knowing."

"Oh, come on," I say, "only God knows everything." That was the right time to zero in on who the voice belonged to. I should have known even then.

We keep walking toward home, the voice and me, and for a while I worry that maybe I offended the voice and it won't come back, but then it starts again, as we cross the street.

"Worrying is a useless habit," the voice says. "I wonder if you have any idea how worrying stops you from seeing all sorts of minor miracles that the world is filled with."

I didn't say anything to that. That's easy for the

voice to say, being Polish and all and not knowing how hard it is to live in New York City and not worry. By then we were next to Mr. Skarbinski's empty lot. And that place had worried me for over a year now. Anyway, I would never have stopped to talk to him that day a year ago, except I heard him use the only Polish swearword I happen to know. His English wasn't too good then, and it hasn't improved much since. It took me quite a while to understand that he intended to turn this miserable empty lot between two buildings into a garden for the neighborhood. The lot was full of garbage, and that first time I saw it he was dragging this sofa to the sidewalk and must have pulled a muscle or something, and that made him swear. Anyway, I helped him with the sofa, and he told me about this dream he had of a garden.

A year later Mr. Skarbinski still can't stop people from dumping their garbage and junk onto that lot. He managed to grow one miserable flower, though. By then it didn't look so hopeless—that lot could have had a future. He had rows of vegetable seeds planted, and they were beginning to sprout. But that was a few months ago, and on this Friday the place looked real bad.

"He reminds me of Job," the voice said to me.

"Rain coming," Mr. Skarbinski said, looking up at the sky. "Good for growing zings."

"Sure," I said.

There were no growing "zings" visible in that place, and besides it was September now, and he had missed his crop another year. What I could see in the lot, which must have been gone over by a bunch of vandals, was a broken bike, two cabinets with one leg each, one broken TV with nothing inside, about a dozen garbage bags with baby diapers spilling out of them, a double-bed mattress, and one half of a chair. That was just the stuff that got tossed out since yesterday.

"Bulbs below," Mr. Skarbinski said, pointing to the junk. "I plant what you call perennials. Come zis year, if possible; not zis year, next year."

Before I knew it, he conned me into helping him drag all that junk to the sidewalk. I had told him about a hundred times that I wasn't going to waste my time on a hopeless job. But it never does any good. He always cons me into helping him. When we're through, he goes over to this beat-up briefcase that he carries around with him, and he takes out two Magic Markers and four pieces of white cardboard.

"You write here, good English, about garden, so people know and read," Mr. Skarbinski says to me. He's learning English all along, so at least I don't spend a lot of time figuring out what his next con is going to be anymore.

"What do you want me to write?" I ask, but even before he can answer I hear my voice saying, "Living Things Need Tender Loving Care," and I came up with "This Is Your Neighborhood Garden" and "Enjoy It, Don't Destroy It," and Mr. Skarbinski's contribution was "And No Disturb Nozzing." He nailed each cardboard to a two-by-four, and we planted them exactly three feet apart.

"Why do you think the garden will never grow?" the voice asked as I stood looking at those signs, feeling sad.

Before I could answer my voice, a bag full of papers conked me on the head and Mr. Skarbinski was yelling up toward the apartment where it came from, and then he grabs me by the sleeve, and his face is very serious, and I know he's got something important to say. We sit down, side by side, on the curb and he says, "Enemy not people. Enemy here." He points to the street, then the sidewalk. "Enemy seemant."

I don't understand, and am about to ask him what he means, when the voice says, "He means cement. And he's right."

Mr. Skarbinski touches the sidewalk with his gnarled fingers and repeats "seemant," and when I correct him he grins and says, "Cement, it makes people heart hard." He smiles. He doesn't have too many teeth left, and I always get depressed whenever he smiles, but this time I just smile back at him and say that he's right.

"Little piece in city with no seemant," Mr. Skarbinski says, growing serious again, "it makes hearts soft. One day maybe all seemant in city go away and eart' be under feet. Den people good and soft in heart."

I shake my head, because I don't believe that will ever happen unless we get blasted by a bomb, but before I can say anything discouraging to Mr. Skarbinski, my voice pipes up, "The difference between

20

him and you is that he's got faith and you need it. Learn from him, Christian."

"Dis garden," Mr. Skarbinski is saying, "important. Like Columbus. I discover eart' in city, and odder people they will discover heart. You help my dream. You good boy."

Instead of learning anything from him, I can't help feeling worried about him. I know he doesn't have any money and won't take anything like welfare or unemployment because, he says, "You let government give you, and you not know what dey take from you. Dey keep deir money, I keep my soul." And he spent a lot on the markers and the cardboard and the two-by-fours. His pants are held up with safety pins, and he keeps being so darn impractical!

I've been feeling more and more personally responsible for things. Like hungry people. Each time I eat anything, I worry about them and feel guilty that I'm eating and they're not. So as I walked away from Mr. Skarbinski, I was worrying about him and feeling guilty about all that money he spent, when the voice says, "I don't remember appointing you the worry king of New York City."

And that gets me mad, so I sort of shout, "Well, I don't like it, worrying all the time."

"You must be a pessimist," the voice says to me.

"I try not to be," I say, feeling stupid.

"With a little faith and trust you can be an optimist, you know," the voice says. "Let me tell you a story. If you've heard it before, just stop me. There were once two boys who got locked into two separate rooms. One boy's room was filled with the most marvelous toys and games and treasures of one kind and another. The other boy's room had nothing in it except horse manure.

"So after a little while they opened the door to the lucky boy's room and they found him looking very sad, just standing among all those toys and games and treasures. 'What's wrong, why do you look so sad?' they asked him. 'I'm afraid of touching any of this stuff because I'm sure to break something if I do,' the boy said. They opened the door to the other boy's room, and he was all smiles, standing there with the horse manure. 'Why are you so happy?' they asked him. And he said, 'With all this manure, there must be a pony around here somewhere.' Now, one boy was a pessimist and the other an optimist. Which one do you think was happier, and which would you rather be?"

I say I'd rather be an optimist, except I must have been born a pessimist.

"An optimist is a person who sees meaning in everything and guesses that everything makes sense," the voice says.

"That's hard for me, to make sense of evil and pain and things like that. I just wish there was someone who could teach me to make sense of everything."

"Let's take Jesus," the voice says. "He certainly tried to teach about sense and meaning. There is meaning to the crucifixion and sense to the resurrection. Without one there would not have been the other. He talked about unconditional love, and limitless trust, and complete faith in his Father. And he came to teach. As far as I remember, you learned about him, didn't you?"

That was some time ago, when I was eight and studied for my first Communion. I suddenly realize that I wasn't born a pessimist at all. When I was a little kid, I was an optimist. I was going to ask the voice what I should do to get back to the way I used to be, but we were getting close to the apartment house where Mr. Brown, our doorman, was standing, and I didn't want him to see me yakking away with someone invisible.

"Would you like it better if I were seen?" the voice asks then.

And without thinking I said, "I sure would."

Then I hear the voice say, "It's not going to be a regulation miracle," and I feel a tug on my sleeve, and I look down, and there is this scrawny-looking Puerto Rican kid, maybe about eight years old, standing next to me. His forehead is badly bruised, and he's got a black eye, and his neck looks hurt. He's wearing short pants, and his legs look all battered up, and the hand that touches me has a real bad burn.

I feel terrible and think I am going to cry or call for help, when he says, "Don't worry, Christian," and it's the voice. "I borrowed a body. It doesn't hurt anymore."

Mr. Brown was getting a taxi for Mrs. Richardson and didn't see the boy appear, and I am still looking at the kid, when all his hurts seem to melt away, and he just looks scrawny, but there are no more bruises on him or burns.

"Where did he come from?" Mr. Brown says to me, pointing to the kid as he goes to open the front door.

I don't know what made me say what I said next. "Nowhere and everywhere."

And I am thinking what a strange thing to say, while Mr. Brown is asking the kid, "What's your name, kid?"

"God," the kid says.

I am just standing there, my mouth wide open, my ulcer inflating, and my hair falling out, and Mr. Brown is winking at me, and out of the side of his mouth he whispers, "They're getting up in the world. Used to be they called their kids 'Jesus.'" He's pronouncing it the way the Spanish people do, *Heysoos*. Then he turns to the kid and says, "Well, hi, there, God."

And the kid says, "Hi, Mr. Brown."

I am not proud of what I did next. I tried to lose the kid. I walked inside the lobby real fast and hoped he'd stay outside. Just then the elevator appeared, and the kid rushed in yelling, "Up!"

Mr. Caparelli, our elevator man, put his arm in front of the door and said, "Where do you think you're going?"

I really felt panicky and was going to be like St. Peter and deny God right then and there, when the kid said, "I am with him," and he points at me.

Mr. Caparelli turns to me and asks, "He with you?"

The kid is looking at me with this strange look, and

I feel suddenly really ashamed for having wanted to ditch God. I mean, I've always believed in him and all.

"He sure is," I said.

When we got to my floor, I looked at the kid and he was smiling. And I just had to smile back. And it was only then, when I saw him smile and smiled back at him, that it happened!

I got this fantastic surge of great feeling inside. It was like nothing I've ever felt before. It was as if all the happiness in the world suddenly got together and went inside my body. It was like I was expanding, growing bigger than the earth and taller than the stars. The thing was, usually I would be scared, or worried, or embarrassed by something so new. But I wasn't any of those things. Maybe it was the realization that I was someone with a whole bunch of ancestors behind me who'd rather die than deny their voices. I guess it was finally understanding this special thing I was given, this gift, not getting just some saint or martyr of my own but getting God!

I began to cry. I just sat down, right there in the foyer, and started to bawl like a baby, and he sat down beside me. I knew that I'd never been happier in my life. I had this crazy thought that everything was going to turn out for the best, that everything was O.K. with the whole world. It felt as if a huge wave of something warm and wonderful hit me. It was like maybe I suddenly understood that God was real, and he was with me, holding my hand and looking sort of silly in his beat-up sweater and short pants.

And then he said something really wonderful:

"Do you know that's how you're supposed to feel all the time?"

I thought he must have been joking, because it was like being crazy or something, and you couldn't feel that way, or else men in white coats would be coming to get you.

"There is a word in your language," he said then, "that fits perfectly what you've experienced. The word is 'beatitude.' "

Anyway, when we walked into my apartment, there was the meeting of WOW. Ever since my mom joined this organization of Women of the World, I had to practically live with them, and it used to scare me, listening to them scheme and plan. I was worried that they weren't fooling but would, one day, parachute into the White House rose garden and take the President hostage, just like they kept saying they would.

Anyway, just as we came in, my mom was saying, "The motion before us is that God is a woman. Do I hear a second?"

We were out in the hall, and when God hears that, he walks right into the living room and says, "Hold it! I'm neither man nor woman. God cannot be defined in human terms."

They ignored him. It was like they didn't hear him or see him.

"I second the motion," says Ms. Johanssen and Mrs. White together.

"It is so moved," my mother says, and God just backs out of the room and suddenly looks very sad and tired. Ordinarily I would worry like crazy about what they did and how they ignored him, and if I were my old self I would worry about how he could have thrown a thunderbolt into the room, or even flooded it or something, because I used to think that God was very big on punishments.

"If I had appeared before those women as a ball of light or a burning bush," he said, "they'd have paid attention."

We were in my room by then, and he lay down on the bed and looked up at the ceiling.

"I've never wanted people to think that all I was good for was to do tricks."

I was feeling really bad. We must have been such a disappointment to him all along. But now God wanted to talk.

"You never asked me," he said then, "how come I look as I do." I never asked him because I was trying to forget about those bruises that disappeared. "At that moment when you said that you'd just as soon see me," he went on, "this little boy, José Martinez, was dying. He had lived for seven years without being loved by anyone but me. So he was very special to me. He was beaten and burned and grievously abused by his parents. You know, Christian, of all the miracles I've made, I'm most proud of children. And there is something so terribly wrong when my most precious miracles get hurt."

"Why don't you strike dead those people who

hurt children?" I asked him.

"For many reasons, but the principal reason is that I've allowed people free will, to do right or do wrong. And I've allowed evil to exist, just as I've allowed good. I will judge and punish those people who are evil in my own time."

He fell asleep then, and I watched him for a while, and then I got down my dictionary and looked up that word. *Beatitude,* it said, *a state of utmost bliss.* I was in it for a while, but I was no longer in it now. I fell asleep thinking about God saying that we're supposed to feel that way all the time.

Nothing really big happened next. God woke up and said he was hungry, and we went to the kitchen. I introduced him to Mrs. Murphy as God, and they smiled and shook hands, and Mrs. Murphy didn't even bat an eye over the fact that he was God. She just accepted him as if it was the most natural thing. She doesn't get upset about things that would upset most people.

"How would you like some milk, God?" she asked him.

"I'd rather try a Coke," God said.

"It's bad for your teeth," Mrs. Murphy said, but she got him a Coke anyway, and some potato chips, and made him a ham sandwich and asked him when he ate the last time, and he said almost two thousand years ago.

Mrs. Murphy was telling God about old Mr. Salvatore Petroccini. He's my only adult friend. Anyway, I used to be worried about how they might get married, Mrs. Murphy and Mr. Petroccini, and what I'd do without her. She means a lot to me, Mrs. Murphy does. She's brought me up ever since I was a baby. Without her I'd probably be a nut locked up in some insane asylum.

Mrs. Murphy was like my teacher. At least, if she didn't teach me anything else, she taught me how to be prejudiced. Like I'm prejudiced against appearances because they don't tell you anything but lies. And I'm prejudiced against people who don't figure things out for themselves but rely on somebody else to tell them how to think. And me and Mrs. Murphy always hated conformists. Mrs. Murphy once told me that I had to stand out from the crowd because "crowds are a bad lot."

My parents never taught me anything that I can remember.

I'd been feeling miserable about my parents not getting along and worrying that I was the cause of it all. They never fight, but I wish they would. I used to wish I were a small kid again, when my father seemed happy working as a diamond cutter. Before my mother went back to school and took up psychology.

It was all downhill for them after that. And when she joined WOW, he locked himself up in that guest room. I haven't seen him for months. Before that happened, we used to meet only at dinner, and there was a lot of "Tell your mother . . ." "Inform your father . . ." stuff going on, and I was like an unpaid messenger between them. I was sort of relieved when he decided to stay in the guest room. Anyway, all that's like water under the bridge, except, sitting there in the kitchen and hearing Mrs. Murphy and God talk, I was thinking that none of that, which used to be so important, was important any more. I didn't feel, for the first time in my life, responsible for them. I mean, I felt free and not guilty any more.

Right after I realized that there had been this terrific change in me, Mrs. Murphy told me that she'd read the letter I got from my grandfather.

"I'm a snoop, so hang me," she said. "I'm part of this family. I also read letters your grandpa used to send your father, about telling you about the voice you'd be hearing." She looked toward God and shook her head. "I didn't think it would be God himself. And I didn't figure that you'd get to see him."

Then God had to go to the bathroom, so we talked about him behind his back. I asked Mrs. Murphy what she thought of my mother and her friends not even seeming to hear God when he told them that he was not a woman, and she said, "Some people can't take in the idea of God, so they sort of step aside, even when he's around, and don't bother noticing him."

"But how could you accept him so easily?" I asked her.

"I figured," she said, "that it was about time he came, at least for a visit."

"It doesn't bother you that he came as a Puerto Rican kid?"

"Well, that was his choice and not yours, wasn't it?" She thought for a while and then said, "You know, I bet he could have chosen anyone, either dying or not, but he chose that kid. Why?"

"Because," I said, "the kid wasn't loved by anyone but him."

"I'd like to meet your father," is what God said after he came back from the bathroom and when he was all through with his Coke, his potato chips, and his ham sandwich.

I figured, him being God, he knew all about my father. My father actually had been acting very strange ever since my mother went back to college and studied to be an abnormal psychologist. When she wrote this thesis on their marriage, his hands began to shake so bad he stopped cutting diamonds. Mother becoming a psychologist really freaked him out. He always thought she was analyzing him like a bug on a pin.

Anyway, he's my father and I love him and I hoped God didn't have a bad impression of him. I didn't think my father'd come out or anything, so there wasn't much chance of their meeting, but maybe God pulled a small miracle, because when he knocked, my father opened the door.

I hadn't seen him for months, except through the keyhole. He wasn't looking all that hot, having grown a beard and all.

After he opened the door, he walked over to this beat-up chair and sat down, and we came in, God and me, and sat down on his bed, and nobody said anything for a minute or so.

"I hear you're a diamond cutter," God said.

My father looked miserable. He pulled his old bathrobe around him and said, in this sad voice, "I used to be."

My dad, he was the best diamond cutter in the world, and when I was growing up I was very proud of him. And I felt real bad when he quit doing it.

"Oh, I wish you'd cut a diamond," God says to my father, real innocent, as if he's never seen that before. "That's what I hoped to see, you cutting a diamond, Mr. Wolny."

"I haven't touched my tools in a long time," my father says, and looks down at his hands, but they're not shaking.

Well, anyway, Dad goes straight to his workroom, this room where he used to work, and starts taking out his box of tools and this giant diamond in the rough and sets everything he needs on the bench.

He turns toward God, then, and says, "So, you want to see a diamond cut. I will show you how it's done."

And he starts explaining everything to God, all the things I've always wanted to know about his trade. How it takes "educated guesses" and "guts." And he's saying things like he had this "terrific wrist motion," and that's what made him so good. And then he points to this diamond that is ready to get cut, and he says that he called it the "Star of Poland" and that he was waiting for a special occasion to give it a crack.

It was beautiful to see him do it. Actually this was the very first time I'd seen him cut a diamond. I was so proud of him, and God was filled with admiration too. Then, when he was finished and the diamond lay sparkling on his workbench, my father got up and said he was going to shave and get dressed, but not before he got some things straightened out with his wife.

I'll skip the dinner scene. But neither God, nor I, nor Mother, nor even Mrs. Murphy had a chance to say anything. Father did all the talking. He was pretty marvelous, and funny, as he put himself down as he used to be and painted himself as he was going to be. Then he presented Mother with the diamond he had cut and told her that it was his present because they happened to have been married eighteen years ago today, just in case she had forgotten.

"Marriage, being an institutional form of slavery—" Mother started to say, when he scooped her off her chair and carried her out of the room.

"Will they make it? Will they stay married and happy?" I asked God.

"Oh, Christian, do you want me to be a fortune-teller?" God asked me with a sigh.

"But you know," I said. "You could tell me."

"My vision is a total vision of the soul's progress," God said, "and 'making it' in my language is not the same as in yours. All I can say is that for you to worry about them would be quite useless."

"I'm not worried, not any more. I just wanted to know," I said.

"Trusting is knowing," he said.

God and I watched television together until well past midnight, because he wanted to see one of his favorite movies. It happens to be one of my all-time favorites too—*Whistle Down the Wind.*

Next morning, Saturday, Mrs. Murphy had her hat on while she cooked pancakes for us. She was going to see Mr. Petroccini, and God wanted to come along and so did I. God loved his pancakes. He had two stacks splattered with real Vermont syrup and melted butter, and his chin got all sticky, and as he looked at me he said, "I can see why some people get fat."

I couldn't figure it, whether he didn't know the taste of food, being God and not usually having a body, or whether he was just enjoying Mrs. Murphy's pancakes.

As we were closing the door, we saw this big sign, made by my mother and nailed to the wall, that said, "Meetings of WOW suspended indefinitely," and that made God as happy as it made me and Mrs. Murphy. Then, on the subway, when he saw all the graffiti he actually seemed to like it. Mrs. Murphy and I always worried about how much it cost the city to remove all the names those vandals spray-paint over everything, but he said, "Years ago, people with paint around paid homage to me and we had a Renaissance. Today they're paying homage to themselves and they are breaking the law, yet there are whole industries built on self-glorification and none of them are against the law."

At 59th Street this old bum gets on. He looks as bad as he smells. He's got dried blood all over his face and what looks like vomit on this horrid old shirt he's wearing, and his hands haven't been washed in a hundred years, and he reeks of cheap wine. Anyway, he stumbles and falls down on his knees, and nobody moves except God. He's down on the floor, helping the bum up and sitting him on the seat, and all I can think of is that God might get some disease from him.

Then I get this idea that no matter what happens, the poor bum was touched by God. It's not wasted, God loving us when we don't even know. It's not wasted at all.

Anyway, the bum goes to sleep, putting his head on God's lap.

I've always hated three streets in Manhattan: 42nd Street around Times Square, 34th Street in front of Macy's and Gimbel's, and 14th Street, all of it. Whenever I'm on any of them I get really depressed. But not on that Saturday. When we got out, 14th Street was filled with Puerto Ricans shopping in those miserable discount stores that are all over. It's a family day, Saturday, and there are lots of little kids around, and some of them are playing out on the street while their parents are shopping. This Puerto Rican lady must have thought God was her kid, and she grabbed him by the hand and said something in Spanish. Then God said something in Spanish to her, and she looked really thunderstruck, her mouth open and every-thing. And God leaves her standing there, and I ask him what happened, and he said that she thought he was her son, but he told her that he was her Father.

I got to feeling really ashamed for how dirty the streets looked as we walked toward University Place. I was going back to the way I used to be, feeling personally responsible for all those papers flying around and the spilled garbage. And then this weird thought came to me that if you want to feel good on the inside, you don't so much notice the ugliness on the outside. I looked around and the street didn't look depressing any more. The garbage was still there, and there was a lot of paper flying around, but all that was O.K. with me. Nothing would ruin the day for me now, I said to myself, and smiled this goofy smile, and that's when Mrs. Murphy told me that she was thinking of accepting Mr. Petroccini's marriage proposal, and that was O.K. with me now too. This was sort of a minor miracle, because for a year now I was afraid she'd do it. But everything was O.K.

And then Mrs. Murphy asked God something that I've never given much thought to.

"What happens after death? I mean, when people were married to someone and then remarry? Do they, after death, see both of their mates—I mean, if they get to heaven, that is?"

God was skipping over the cracks in the sidewalk at the time, and we were going right past the window of an antique store that had a statue of Jesus and Mary in it, and God was reflected in the glass, and it seemed incredibly more interesting to me than Mrs. Murphy's question.

"Why don't you answer her?" God said to me.

I didn't know what to say. I knew that Mr. Petroccini was married before and that his wife had died a dozen years ago, and I guess Mrs. Murphy was afraid of running into her in heaven, and also into her own husband, who died when she was only twenty.

"Why can't you answer?" Mrs. Murphy wanted to know.

"Because," God said, "I'd like to hear what Christian might say."

"O.K., Christian, what happens after death?" Mrs. Murphy asks me.

"Well," I began, not knowing what I was going to say next, "I don't think there is such a thing as jealousy in heaven. And I think everybody is comfortable with everybody there, so I don't think you'll have any problems with Mrs. Petroccini."

"Sounds good to me," said God.

"I also feel," I added, because Mrs. Murphy looked sort of doubtful, "that being in heaven is like being so full of happiness and"—I smiled at God—"and beatitude, that nobody has much time to worry about who they were married to back on earth. I think they're into something else, bigger even than marriage."

"You're getting there," God said, and I hoped he meant not only getting it right but getting toward heaven.

Before we got to Mr. Petroccini's apartment, we stopped and bought him some flowers. They cost Mrs. Murphy five dollars for just a little bunch of daisies and goldenrod, I think.

"I thought I made enough flowers so they wouldn't cost so much," God said.

Mr. Petroccini lives in this run-down apartment house that's squeezed between two factories, on 10th Street between University and Astor Place. They hadn't gotten around to improving that block at all. It's not too bad a block, as blocks go, but it's not fancy like so many blocks in the Village are now. Anyway, the strange thing about this real narrow building is that there are only old people living in it.

Like Mr. Petroccini says, "We're hanging on here because the rents are low. Somebody seems to have forgotten about this building. There hasn't been an increase in twenty years." He feels that low rent is what keeps all those people from "checking out," which means dying.

What always depressed me about that building was the quality of its garbage. I mean, all those old tenants put their garbage outside their doors, and there isn't much of it, just cans of mostly mackerel, which smells real bad but is cheap. And everybody seems to have cats, and the whole place smells of cat stuff. I also think that a lot of these people in that building can't afford to eat anything but what their cats eat, because there's always so darn many cans of cat food and nothing else spilling out of those little trash bags.

But this time I didn't feel depressed walking up the stairs. I couldn't wait for Mr. Petroccini to meet up with God.

Anyway, we knocked on his door, and he says to come in because he never keeps it locked. He may be the only person in the city who doesn't even have a key to his apartment. He once told me, "You can't keep thieves outta the house with a lock. They break locks. I hope a thief comes in here and I have a talk with him. He won't steal any more."

For somebody his age, Mr. Petroccini sure likes to fool around a lot. He loves the streets, and he often pretends he's a bum and asks for handouts. He says that he learns a lot about strangers that way. Like, a lot of people who don't look scared are really frightened of everything, he says, and he tries to talk them out of being fearful. And a lot are very angry, and he tries to make them laugh. Those who share with him he invites over for a cup of his famous cappuccino. Another thing he likes to do is stand around sidewalk cafés and watch people eat.

"It makes people embarrassed," he says, "to be watched eating. Isn't that strange? With all that pornography around, you'd think people wouldn't be ashamed of being seen doing a clean thing like eating."

He often does research on human nature. He would take out a notepad and pencil and ask eating questions in this Italian accent he likes to put on. He'd ask things like, "You eat-a often? How often? You enjoy? Whatta you feed-a your soul?"

Well, to get back to our visit with Mr. Petroccini, he was lying in bed and had on this crazy-looking bathrobe which he'd made out of a drape he found in somebody's garbage. That's another thing about him. He's a great junk collector. His apartment is filled with all sorts of interesting, useless, but beautiful things. Almost everything has something wrong with it, it doesn't work, or a piece is broken off, or something like that. That's what attracted Mrs. Murphy to him in the first place, because she keeps breaking things all the time.

Actually that's how we met him, at this garbage can, because Mrs. Murphy broke a can opener and didn't want to discard it near home, and we took a subway all the way to the Village. Anyway, as Mrs. Murphy was throwing away that electric can opener, there was Mr. Petroccini saying that he collects broken things, but that electric gadgets are not what interests him. She said that he could come to our apartment and help himself, because almost everything she ever dusted got broken. But he said that wouldn't do at all, because he's only interested in things people have discarded, things they no longer keep around.

"I make a connection between broken, discarded things and old people, you see," he told us. But we didn't see. Not then. Not before we got to know him. What he's doing is "philosophically correct," as he says. He's taking care of what gets old and useless.

Mr. Petroccini has a great respect for the law. He says that's what makes us civilized. Laws do. The only

43

thing is, he thinks God's laws are better than people's. When they're contradicting each other, he feels we've got to choose God's laws, not people's.

Anyway, there he was lying down, and Mrs. Murphy looked real scared, because she thought he might be sick.

"I thought I'd die," Mr. Petroccini says. "I've been reading this article and it said that people who went over the brink of death had this great feeling of happiness, so I was trying for it."

"You're a crazy old man," Mrs. Murphy says and pecks him on the cheek. "Look who we brought to you. This is God. God, this is Mr. Salvatore Petroccini."

They shook hands.

"You're awfully young-looking for being so old," Mr. Petroccini says to God.

"Yes, I'm older than I look," says God.

Then Mr. Petroccini jumps out of bed and starts brewing his cappuccino. I hate coffee, except when he makes it. He always goes through this routine of brewing that coffee in this strange-looking contraption that he himself invented, but this time he can't manage, he's that excited, and he finally lets Mrs. Murphy attend to it.

"I can't pretend that this isn't the greatest thing that ever happened to me," he says. "Having God in this forsaken place." Then he bends to God, who's standing in the middle of the room, and says, "Can I touch you?" And God nods his head, and Mr. Petroccini touches him very gently on the head.

"I just knew you'd come around one day. But what I thought was that I wouldn't be around for the Messianic age."

"This isn't it," God says. "Not yet."

Mr. Petroccini is nervous, I know, and starts moving books and newspapers and magazines off the sofa so that we can sit down. And when we do, he goes on. "This dying business, it's hard to do unless it's your time to go. But that article, God, was really something. When I was reading it I thought that surely the Holy Spirit had a hand in it. It had a dozen interviews with people who had clinically died, and all of them felt this tremendous elation—"

"Beatitude," I say, and God smiles at me.

"Now, God, tell me," Mr. Petroccini says, "is that something temporary, just as you die, or does it go on forever?"

"It goes on forever if you happen to end up in heaven," I say.

"Dying is the perfect way to let go of one thing and start on something new," Mrs. Murphy says.

"You've never experienced death, have you, God?"

"All reports of his death have been premature," Mrs. Murphy says.

Mr. Petroccini doesn't seem to notice that God has not answered him directly yet. "I think we're just taking our first steps into knowing about death. Is that right on time, on your schedule, for us to stop fearing death and accept it with joy?"

"I hope this won't lead us into mass suicides," says Mrs. Murphy as she passes us some cookies that she's baked.

"There is nothing to fear, right, God?"

"Not if you think you deserve happiness," I say.

I have this great feeling that we are doing what God wants us to do, answer for him. It's sort of like a test, for us, of what we might have figured out, and I was willing, without feeling ashamed or anything, to share it with Mr. Petroccini. But Mr. Petroccini just won't let up talking to God directly. He's got this unique chance to do what he's wanted to do all along, and he's going for it.

"Who, would you say, are the greatest thinkers in the world?" he asks, and before anyone has a chance to answer, he adds, "I bet you're going to say Aristotle, Socrates, and Thomas Aquinas, right?"

"That's the lineup of the major league," God says. "But personally I like Jacob Horowitz."

"Who's Jacob Horowitz?" Mr. Petroccini asks and looks stunned. He prides himself on knowing all "the people in the world who have made a difference," as he often says. "I've never heard of him."

"Very few people have heard of him," God says. "He lived in a small village in Poland at the turn of this century. He tried to be a farmer and had a very hard time of it. He used to talk to me a lot, and I liked the way he thought."

"But can you compare him with Aquinas?"

48

"I can, but maybe you couldn't. He was a simple man."

God is busy eating the cookies now and sort of nods his head, and I look around and there is Mrs. Murphy cleaning up the place. Whenever we visit she does that. She doesn't like dirt around, and Mr. Petroccini's place never lacks for it.

Mr. Petroccini pulled his chair in front of God and leaned his face in his hands and concentrated on his next question. He has a very good face. You could read it like a book because of all those wrinkles. He is a fellow worrier, except he calls himself a "secret worrier" and is always preaching at me for being too young to worry. "I didn't start worrying until I was into my fifties," he told me once.

"Now, let's take life," Mr. Petroccini was saying. "How come we keep fouling it up?"

"Speak for yourself," said Mrs. Murphy from behind him.

"Listen, God, you could stop all that messing around we do. We could use a flood, right about now, or some pestilence—"

"I don't think God sent pestilence," I said. "Only the flood, and only once."

"Right," God says to me.

"Are you proud of anything we've been doing down here?" is what Mr. Petroccini asks next.

"Not a day goes by," God says, "that I am not proud of someone."

"Right now, at this very minute, who are you most proud of?" Mr. Petroccini asks.

"Him," God says and points at me. I was dying to ask what made him proud of me, but I didn't get a chance.

"No, I mean, historically speaking? What are we doing right, collectively, at this very minute?"

God has to think about that, and that surprises me, because I thought he never had to take time out to think.

"Maybe," he says, "all that airing that goes on."

"You mean, on TV and newspapers and things? The way we know now about all the evil that goes on, like child abuse, which always went on, but we talk about it, and abortions and things like that?"

"Yes," God says.

"But how about summarizing it all for us?" Mr. Petroccini says, drumming his fingers like crazy on the coffee table and making his cup of cappuccino jump around in its saucer.

"Wisdom in a nutshell?" God says. "You wouldn't want that, would you?"

"I would," I say, and am immediately ashamed of myself.

"I wouldn't, on second thought," Mr. Petroccini says. "That was a dumb request. And I'm ashamed of myself."

"Me, too," I say.

God was smiling and enjoying the cappuccino. "Don't feel bad," he tells us. "Whenever anyone talks to me, that's like a regulation question. After all, who else would know how to answer it?"

We all laughed, then, and agreed that God and I

would take in a movie, and Mrs. Murphy would stay around to settle "the matrimonial question," as she put it.

We ended up in this theater that had a double bill, *The Maltese Falcon* and *The Big Sleep*. I'm a movie freak, and I couldn't wait to know how God felt about it. I was afraid he might say it's a waste of time. God told me at one point that of all men's inventions, he thought maybe he liked movies the best, and, though I didn't ask him, I figured that maybe in heaven he's got himself this private projection room in which he sees them, or maybe he doesn't have to have a private projection room at all. He just might be seeing them as we see them, in theaters and on TV in our living rooms. I always hoped that if I got to heaven I wouldn't miss movies.

God was some movie fan, sitting deep in his chair, with his feet sort of halfway up, and munching on his popcorn.

My parents weren't there when we came back to the apartment. Father had left me a note that said he had "abducted" my mother to New Jersey. "We don't know when we'll be back. Make your friend feel at home."

When Mrs. Murphy came back, she told us that they'd decided, she and Mr. Petroccini, to get married next week and asked God if he could attend their wedding. And he said that he was always at weddings, and then added, "But I usually skip the divorces."

We both fell asleep watching TV, and would you believe it? God snored! Not very loudly or anything, but he snored nevertheless. I woke up in the middle of the night and heard him!

Sunday God wanted to go to church.

I usually go to the eleven o'clock Mass at St. Francis', right across the street. Father Williams is the one who says it. He likes to talk about God, during his sermons, as if God were a football coach and we were the players on his winning team. I never could figure out if Father Williams was supposed to have been the assistant coach, or just the quarterback. I used to go to the nine o'clock Mass, which is always said by Father Brown. Father Brown doesn't like to fool around with God. He talks about the devil. He always paints him so shoddy, so mean, and so stupid that nobody wants to have anything to do with him.

You can take God to church, but you can't know what the church will make out of God. God liked it. I mean, he liked the way St. Francis' looked. There were flowers all over, because this happened to have been the anniversary of the Ladies of the Altar Society.

God wanted to sit in the first pew. Now the first pew, during the eleven o'clock Mass, the first pew on the left, is reserved for Mr. and Mrs. Jerome P. Fitzpatrick and their family. Anybody who goes to that Mass knows that. The Fitzpatricks have sat there maybe for centuries, and there is just enough space for all of them. Besides Mr. and Mrs. Jerome Fitzpatrick and their four daughters, there are Robert and James, their two sons, who are older than I, and both of them used to gang up on me at school and beat me up. They are twins, and they used to really lord it over the younger kids. And most of the time they'd get away with it, because one would blame the other. They both look like their father. Now, Mr. Fitzpatrick, curiously enough, isn't an ugly man. He's very big and has, as one nun once said, "very strong features." But so do the girls. They are all big and have their father's strong features, but on their faces those features don't look so good. And the other person, besides them, is Mr. Fitzpatrick's mother.

She is like the queen of the whole parish. She's always the first to answer during Mass, and she's always the first to stand, and to sit, and to kneel. And her voice is about the loudest in church. Old Mrs. Fitzpatrick is about the tallest woman I've ever seen. If she wasn't so uppity, she'd make a great basketball player.

Anyway, none of the Fitzpatricks had arrived when God and I sat in their pew. I knew we'd be in trouble, but who was I to tell God where to sit in his own house?

As far as I knew there was no law forbidding anybody from sitting in the Fitzpatrick pew during the eleven o'clock Mass.

I am saying all this, because I want you to know that I was plenty scared. But there was this other thing that took my mind off the problem, and that was the question, Would God pray and who would he be praying to?

Before getting into the pew he did exactly what I did—he knelt and bowed his head—but I figure that was the kid, José, doing it, not God, because he wouldn't be bowing to himself. Then he sat down and closed his eyes, and I didn't know if he was praying or not. And then the Fitzpatricks started to troop in. Old Mrs. Fitzpatrick was first. She gave me this dirty look, like she thought I was crazy to be alive, and started pushing against me, going sideways, like a crab, and I was pushing against God, and I didn't even realize when I got to the end of the pew and pushed him right off the bench, and he fell.

That made me really mad.

"You pushed God right out of his seat," I said to old Mrs. Fitzpatrick. "That's about the crummiest thing anybody could do."

I was going to help him up, then, but he was already up, dusting himself.

"As you very well know, young man," old Mrs. Fitzpatrick is saying to me in this puffed-up way she has, "we've sat in this pew for generations, and I will not have God or anyone else unseat us."

God grabs my hand and pulls me to the pew behind the Fitzpatricks, and then Father Williams is coming out of the sacristy, and halfway to the altar he booms out, "In the name of the Father and of the Son and of the Holy—"

"Amen," old Mrs. Fitzpatrick says real loud, before he has a chance to finish.

I think God was trying hard not to laugh when Father Williams was booming out his sermon.

". . . and that great coach in the sky is keeping an ever-watchful eye over those who foul up the team effort. And on that final day of reckoning he'll take the letters away from those who didn't try their hardest."

When he was through I leaned over to God and asked, "How did you like the commercial he gave you?"

"I'm afraid I'll be a real disappointment to him when we meet," God said.

When the time comes to shake hands, the Fitzpatricks, I know, won't even turn around. They will just shake hands among themselves, like always.

It was then that God left our pew and began to shake hands with the people behind us. I heard him say, "My peace be with you," and "Pass it on," as he went from pew to pew, down the whole length of the church and then back toward the altar.

Father Williams is just waiting to continue Mass, and at first he groans, then he glares, and then, slowly, little by little, he starts to relax, and finally he's smiling. It happens the same way with all the Fitzpatricks. At first they all turn around, looking absolutely furious and indignant, especially old Mrs. Fitzpatrick, and then they begin to break out in smiles.

That was some miracle, because in all the years I've known them, I've never seen one of them ever smile before. And God just continues on his way, down the other aisle, and up again, and when he gets to the first pew, where the Fitzpatricks are sitting, they've got their hands outstretched, and he has to shake hands with them all.

And then, when it was time for Communion, they let him go first! And he received Communion, and Father Williams passes on to God the hosts, and it is he who distributes Communion to everyone. And you know what—everyone had to kneel, because God, being so short, couldn't reach up to them.

I thought God would be mobbed after Mass and that people would want his autograph or something, but it didn't happen. When the Mass ended, it was like the miracle was over. The Fitzpatricks pushed their way past us, not even looking at God, and nobody wanted to know who he was or anything, and Father Williams didn't come out of the sacristy on the run to have a personal encounter with him. And I thought that maybe none of this had happened, maybe I had imagined it all. And I was getting very depressed as we were walking toward Central Park, where God wanted to go, when he says, "Do you mind if I give you one piece of advice?"

"Yeah," I say. "I mind if it's only one piece. I need a lot."

"You'll learn by yourself what you need to learn. But one piece of advice you could have."

I wait, and then he says, "Well, let's say that you arrive at a point in your life when you know in your heart that the earth is full of my goodness. Let's say that it becomes like your personal truth, a fact for you. Now, knowing this, are you still going to worry about other people not knowing this?"

"Sure," I say. "Knowing the real truth, I'd want everyone else to know it."

"So you'd want to do something about it, rather than just worry about it?"

"Well . . ." I wasn't sure what he meant.

"It seems to me you worry instead of doing something about what worries you."

"You're right. But maybe that's because I'm just a kid."

"I know that. You being a kid of eleven. But all that worrying will take your time from enjoying the knowing. Don't you see that, Christian?"

I thought about it, and of course he was right. And then before I even had a chance to think on this, I say, "When I grow up I'll become your priest."

I thought he would be really happy. I was.

"Don't you want me to become a priest?" I ask him.

"That's in the future," he said. "I want you to deal with the present and stop worrying. I'd like you to work on your faith and your trust in me and on joy already experienced, and not put worries in your path."

"O.K.," I said. "But I just thought that—"

"If you decide to become a priest, it will be a man's decision, not a boy's."

"Well, that's the whole problem. When you're a kid, all you can do is worry. Because when you're a kid, you can't do anything."

"How wrong you are!" is what he said then.

I wanted to ask him what he meant, what I could do, but I didn't. I needed patience, I thought.

We walked toward the merry-go-round at the zoo. Two ladies asked us if we'd take their little boys on the merry-go-round, and they handed us four tickets.

And right after our ride I lost him. One moment he was right near me, and the next he wasn't. I looked all over for him, and a few times I thought I saw him, but each time it was some other kid. I thought he went back to ride the merry-go-round and I hung around there for a while getting dizzy, and then I walked to the zoo and back again to the merry-go-round.

It was like a nightmare. I'd call out to him:

"God, where are you?"

Some people who heard me yell for him gave me advice. Like one lady said:

"Seek, and you shall find him."

And an older man said:

"I'm happy to see one young punk interested in God instead of dope."

But I was really scared by then. I couldn't find him anywhere. I began to cry.

I had to sit down and collect my thoughts and feelings. It took me quite a while before I stopped being frantic. I realized that he might have disappeared and that I would never see him again. I knew that it should not change anything I learned while I was with him. And yet I still had to find him. I got up and began to search for him again.

When I saw him he was sitting under a tree with

two junkies, and they were crying. I just stood there, crying like crazy, happy that he had not gone away.

I found out how sad God could be. I wanted to take his sadness away, but I didn't know how.

"They too have been abused by their parents."

That's all I knew. He didn't tell me more.

Just before we left the park, we sat down on a patch of grass. He looked so tired. His eyes, which are usually so bright, were clouded. For a long time he didn't say anything. I tried to think of something to cheer him up, but I couldn't.

There was a small flower lying nearby that someone had stepped on, and it was dead, just drying up, and he picked it up, and I thought it would spring back to life at his touch, but it didn't.

I am going to skip about playing chess with God later that night. By Monday morning I was feeling real bad about having to go to school and leave him, but he said he'd walk with me.

Anyway, we were in front of my school, and I was about to ask God what he was going to do while I was in school, when he tells me that he's coming along. I mean, how was I going to explain to my teachers about him hanging around? I actually didn't want him to come to school with me. I'm ashamed of saying this, but I really wished he wouldn't. I didn't say anything, though I was going to get into trouble for sure.

I was getting nervous about that, about him being

with me, when he says, "I won't talk. I'll let you do the talking for me."

Well, that's swell, I thought, that's just swell. Thank you, God.

There I go again. Worried just as I used to be before he came into my life, but this time worried about him. About God! And he must have known it, that I was about to blow everything, going back to the way I was.

That's when he told me today was going to be my "moment of truth." He told me that, like a bull-fighter, I would have my moment of truth, and I would know at the end of the day more about myself and what I was really like. And he said I should not fear. He told me he had figured me for someone who could do his work, here on earth, and if I was going to get all uptight on the job, then he must have been wrong.

"God can't be wrong," I told him.

"But I can be premature. You might not be ready yet," he said. "I won't force you into anything, because it has to come from you."

"What?" I ask.

"Being willing to go in there with me, speak for me."

"But you won't disappear or anything like that?" I ask. I really needed him around, if this was going to be such a very important day.

"No, I won't disappear, but you might wish me to."

"No, I won't," I said and felt that I wasn't lying.

"Let's go, God," I said, and we walked into the school building.

My first class on Monday is Mr. Gallegos' Social Studies class. Everyone was already in class, doing the usual goofing off, shuffling papers, getting rowdy, yawning all over the place, and flipping spitballs at each other, while Mr. Gallegos was having his cup of coffee and trying not to pay attention to anything around. It takes him awhile to wake up, like ten minutes, before taking roll call.

Anyway, he hasn't gotten around to the roll call yet when me and God walk in and sit in the back row. Philomena Garcia is the only one there in the back, waiting for me as usual, and the first thing she says to me is, "You can't bring this kid in here."

And I say to her, "I sure can. This is God."

And she starts laughing. Nobody else is paying any attention, because they're still busy messing around among themselves, and Mr. Gallegos' nose is deep into this giant mug of coffee.

"Why are you laughing?" I ask her.

"Because that's José Martinez, the dummy who lives in my building, that's why."

"You knew him?" I ask.

"Sure," she says. "He never goes out or anything because he can't talk and can't do nothing else either. He's brain damaged or something."

I didn't know what to do next. I mean I didn't want old Philomena to spoil the whole day for us, so I said to her, "Listen, he's God, and I'd appreciate it very much if you just didn't say you knew him or anything. José Martinez is dead, but God is alive. Please don't say anything at all."

"If I keep quiet, will you go out with me on a date this week?"

I didn't have time to promise her, because Mr. Gallegos is ready to take roll call. He raps the ruler against the desk and starts off at about a thousand miles an hour, "AdamsBarriganBrownChaparellChavez . . ."

Anyway, the moment Mr. Gallegos is through with the roll call, Philomena Garcia stands up and says, real loud, "Christian brought God to school."

And Mr. Gallegos looks toward us and then gives this curious smile, and everyone else looks at us, they're all laughing, and down comes the ruler. And suddenly everyone is silent.

"How many of you lunkheads think Christian brought God to school this morning?"

Not a hand goes up, except mine.

"Now, let me ask you this," Mr. Gallegos says, walking back and forth in front of his desk. "Who can give me a reason why Christian couldn't have brought God to school?"

"Because Christian ain't got any friends in high places," says Freddy Wallace, and he gets a few laughs for that. But old Philomena Garcia springs to my defense.

"He does too," she says.

Down comes the ruler. "Who else has a reason?" Mr. Gallegos asks.

"Because if the kid was God, he'd disappear," Robby Barrigan says. And then he adds in a lower voice, "He wouldn't be caught dead in this lousy school."

After that, everybody had something to say. It was O.K. with them to have God there, if only he would do some tricks and magic. They wanted everything, from making it rain inside to having it be Friday instead of Monday. Kelly's girl, Irma, wanted Kelly's zits to clear up. And Philomena said that she'd believe the kid was God if I asked her to marry me.

I was working hard at not getting depressed.

But Mr. Gallegos kept on with his "exploration," as he called it, and then tried to make everyone define God. Nobody would volunteer, so he called on different kids and just stood there, tapping his ruler against the desk until they came up with something. And then wrote what he got on the blackboard. This is what it looked like:

God equals:

perfect (this came from me because I wanted them to get started and nobody was getting started)
can stop wars (from Michael Chavez)
invisible (this from Philomena)
spirit (from Freddy Wallace)
can stop people doing bad things (from Jim Grossi, who often comes to school with a black eye)
can punish you after death (from Maggie Shneider)

63

hates swearing (from Mary Thorpe, who hates
  swearing)
old (this again from Philomena, because we waited
  so long for the next volunteer)
and

real (from me, because there weren't any more)

Well, that was the whole problem in a nutshell, I
guess. God wasn't real to them.

Mr. Gallegos tried to keep this exploration rolling
along, and he asked next, "What are God's greatest
accomplishments?"

And Philomena said right away, "Not looking so
beat up." But nobody except the three of us understood that.

"Not striking us dead right this minute," said
Freddy Wallace.

"Inventing Coke," said someone up front.

"Creating everything at the beginning," said Jim
Grossi.

"Coming down to us as Jesus," said Charlie Peterson.

"Loving us," said Maggie Shneider.

And that was it. Except Mr. Gallegos then came up
to where we sat and said to God, "What's your name,
kid?"

And I said, "God."

"You'll get into trouble before the day's over," said
Mr. Gallegos and turned on his heels. He then read

to us from our text and gave us our assignment. Then the bell rang and I felt really disappointed, because nobody even looked back at God. Nobody came up to ask him anything. A couple of kids sneered at us as they went out. Only Charlie Peterson, Jim Grossi, and Maggie Shneider hung around as we went to our next class. They were just behind us, like bodyguards. They didn't look at God, though. They had their heads down, as if they were ashamed or something, but they stuck close to us.

Well, let me tell you, I felt that I was blowing the whole thing. There I was, appointed by God to be his spokesman, and I didn't do anything and hardly said anything at all. I started to get angry at myself, walking to Mr. Noble's math class, which was our next class, when God put his hand in mine, and the anger retreated. It was the beginning of our adventure, I thought, and things could only get better.

Mr. Noble's math class is the special "remedial" class mostly for dummies in math, and from our first class only Peterson, Grossi, Shneider, and me were going to be there.

The prettiest girl in Mr. Noble's class is Venus Grace, and she comes right up to me and God and wants to know who the kid is, and when I tell her that he's God, a few kids snicker and laugh, but Venus Grace turns on them and asks, "Why couldn't he be God?"

And this argument starts between the kids who were not in Mr. Gallegos' class and Rossi, Shneider,

Peterson, and Grace. The four were for the idea of God being anybody he chose to be; all the others were against it.

I've never told anyone this, but I have this crush on Venus Grace, but she's never even noticed me before because she's going out with Jericho Horton. I mean, he's super cool, and a word from him is like law all around the school. And ever since Venus Grace came to our school last year, she's been his girl. So right after the argument started, Jericho Horton makes this motion with his hands, which means for everybody to shut up because he's going to have something to say. So everybody quiets down and he takes a minute to think and then he says, "Let the kid speak for himself. Hey, kid, are you God?"

"He is," I say.

"Butt out, I'm asking him," Horton says to me. "Are you or ain't you God?"

"He's not talking today," I say. "He told me I could do the talking for him."

"What's so special about you?" Horton wants to know. "Who appointed you God's mouthpiece?"

A lot of kids are always ready to applaud Horton and get into his good graces. Horton is, by far, the most popular kid in the whole school. And me having a crush on his girl is crazy. Let me tell you, she's some girl! First of all she looks like Carole Lombard, who's my favorite among all the old movie stars. And she's smart—except in math, of course—and very nice. She understands everything. And is kind and so gentle.

Anyway, Venus Grace gives me this searching look right then, while all the kids are saying, "Yeah, what makes you so special, Wolny?" and Venus says, "Christian must be special, or why would God hang around with him?"

I was feeling so pleased that I must have gotten red all over my face, when Lupita Carrion speaks up. She never talks! Everybody thought she was either a deaf-mute or didn't know English. She's the most timid person you've ever seen, but she speaks up now.

"God could be anybody he chooses to be," she says. "And he can choose anybody he wants to speak for him."

"And it's obvious," Maggie Shneider adds, "that he has chosen Christian for his friend."

Horton is waving his hands around again and everybody shuts up, even those who are laughing.

"For starters," Horton says, "if he's God, what's he doing in here? God doesn't belong in school—he belongs in church. If he's God," Horton adds, "what I want to know is how come he allows so many creeps to run around loose getting away with things like murder and abusing little kids and rotten stuff like that?"

Venus Grace is looking at me, and I begin to feel that she's waiting for me to answer. And so is God, because he's looking up at me too.

"It's because of free will," I say. "He gave us free will, and he isn't interfering with that gift."

"O.K.," says Horton. "I buy that. But if he came

back to recall the free will, it would be O.K. with me. He's welcome to it, as far as I'm concerned."

"No," I say, "he didn't come for that. I think he hopes that we will use that free will to choose him, not his enemy."

"His enemy's been playing dirty, and maybe God should do the same," somebody in the back row says.

"Maybe he came," Venus Grace is saying, "because of something special that he wants us to do. Maybe he wants us to help him. Maybe it's getting so bad, with nuclear stuff and all, that he wants us to . . ." She's having trouble figuring this out, and Maggie Shneider is trying to help.

"Maybe we don't know that the time is getting shorter, that we don't have all that much time because somebody might press the button, and God figures we ought to be giving him some thought. I mean, if we're going to destroy his world, he's got something to say about that."

Horton lifts his arms up and spreads them for silence. There was a lot of chitchatting going around while Maggie was talking.

"I just realized something," Horton is saying. And that surprises me, because he's not a kid who'd admit he didn't know everything from the cradle on. "Like maybe all the rotten stuff that's going on isn't his responsibility. It's ours. We ought to clean up our act. Maybe that's why he came, to see that we do it."

That's when Mr. Noble comes in. He's usually late because he likes to smoke in the teachers' lounge. Anyway, some of the kids clue him in on what's been

70

going on. He didn't seem all that interested. He hardly ever seems to be interested in anything, not even in discipline, but the kids aren't ready to go to work. Mr. Noble, as long as the kids don't riot, lets them do pretty much what they want, and he goes to his desk and takes some papers out and starts correcting them. He works nights as a watchman, and I guess he's got to get some sleep sometime, because he does all that teacher work in class. It was so different in Mr. Noble's class. For one thing, it wasn't boring. There was real excitement in the room. I guess the difference was that in Mr. Gallegos' class the kids all wondered "Why?" and in Mr. Noble's remedial math class it was more like "Why not?"

"Hey, Wolny," Horton asks me at one point, "When did God give us this free will as a gift?"

"It must have been in the Garden of Eden," I say. "Adam and Eve, they had everything, including the tree of knowledge. Before they ate of that tree they didn't know that they could want things that God didn't want for them. When they ate that apple, that's when they realized they could disobey God."

Mr. Noble by then is at the blackboard writing a problem for us to solve. He calls this stuff "multiple fractures," but actually they are fractions. And he's turning to the class and calling for a volunteer.

"Can't we forget all that math junk," Jim Rossi wants to know, "and concentrate on God?"

"Yeah." Horton seconds him. "We were just beginning to have a serious discussion here."

Mr. Noble goes to his desk, takes his snuff box from

his pocket, puts his feet on the desk, takes a pinch of snuff, puts it up his nose, and stares right ahead. A couple of years back, Mr. Noble was teaching high school in a real tough neighborhood in the Bronx. They kicked him out because he was sniffing snuff. All the kids who used to be on hard drugs got on snuff too, and some junkie of a mother whose son was no longer a junkie got so mad she got him fired. Ever since then, Mr. Noble has been very cynical about things. Like he once said to me, "We've gone right down Alice's rabbit hole, and the Establishment is having a tea party. The inmates are running the asylum, and all spectators are in danger." When I said I didn't get it, he said, "That's my new philosophy, kid. Take it or leave it."

So, for a while, Mr. Noble is just sitting there looking at us as we're discussing what God could do about our various problems if only he wanted to. And I am thinking that we've slid back from where we were before, feeling responsible about what we do and knowing about free will to mess up. And then suddenly Mr. Noble, after a few mighty sneezes, gets up and says, "All right. How many of you think Christian brought God to school?"

A few hands go up. Mine and Venus Grace's, Charlie Peterson's, Jim Grossi's, Maggie Shneider's, Lupita Carrion's. And then, slowly, Horton raises his hand too. And immediately after, there are more hands going up until all of them are in the air. Mr. Noble is giving us this crooked smile of his, which he always gives us when he's got something up his sleeve.

"I'm sorry to inform you," he says very slow, "that God isn't allowed in school."

You should have heard the racket after he said that, that God wasn't allowed in school. Mr. Noble tries to quiet everybody down, but he can't, and only when Jericho Horton starts waving his hand does everybody shut up at once.

"Would you explain what you just said?" Horton asks.

"God has not been allowed in public schools since the courts kicked him out. And that's the law."

"They kicked God out of school with a law?" Horton wants to know.

Mr. Noble, who once told us that he always wanted to be a lawyer until he found out that there weren't too many who weren't crooks, then gave us this whole explanation of the Supreme Court decision.

"On that day," he said, "I decided not to be a lawyer, so I know what I'm talking about." And then he pauses, sneezes, and slowly says, "So, God will have to go."

"He goes, I go," says Jim Grossi.

"The place you're going is the principal's office," Mr. Noble says then.

Well, not everybody went. Just me and God and Jim Grossi. And then Lupita Carrion, Maggie Shneider, and Charlie Peterson follow us and form

73

like an honor guard for me and God. And before we're halfway to the principal's office, Horton and Venus Grace join us. By then Lupita and Maggie have each taken one of God's hands, and Jim Grossi and Charlie Peterson are talking about what a fight they're going to put up because God should be allowed in school. And Horton joins in and says they could take this thing all the way to the Supreme Court, and then bends over God and says, "I ain't leaving you, God, no matter what. And with Jericho Horton around, you ain't got nothing to fear."

And Venus Grace bends down and kisses God on top of his head and says, "Whither thou goest, I shall go too."

And God is smiling like crazy, and I feel pretty terrific too. Actually, I am getting into this beatitude thing, right there in the corridor, with our new friends probably experiencing the same thing.

Our principal, Mrs. Gallop, has this office that's always guarded by the school secretary, Miss Bueno, and she comes from behind her desk and says she isn't allowing us in until she knows what it's all about. But we don't pay any attention because Horton had already opened the door to Mrs. Gallop's office, and he starts shoving us all inside and then closes the door right in Miss Bueno's face. Then Horton goes straight to Mrs. Gallop's desk, and she hides those nail things she was using in her drawer and begins to look very sternly at us all. The girls are surrounding God, and I don't think she can even see him from where she's sitting, but Horton is saying, "We've got God here with us, see, and what are you going to do about that?"

She's really flustered, because we interrupted her manicure and all, and wants to know what Horton is talking about, and everybody says that we've got God and he isn't going to get kicked out of school, and Horton shoves God in front of her and tells her that the little kid is really God. Mrs. Gallop is really confused, but I can see that God is giving her this big grin.

"What we want to know is," Horton is saying, "are you going to allow God in school or aren't you?"

Anyway, to make it short, she called the child welfare people because she didn't believe God was God but wanted him "identified."

While we were waiting for the people from child welfare to arrive, the principal tried to get us all back into our classes, but Horton wouldn't have any of it.

"How many times in life do you get to spend some time with God in person?" he said. So we all sat together, around God, in the office, and there wasn't much talk. Everybody just wanted to be close to God and to touch him. He got hugged a lot.

Then they all wanted to know what they could do for him, as if they knew he wouldn't be around too much longer. And I felt that way too, that something was going to happen and he'd be taken away from us. So I told them what he had said about little children, how he considered them the best miracle of all and how it hurt him when children were abused. And I told them what he told me about José Martinez,

75

about how he was unloved by everyone, and how he died of abuse.

We stuck by God when those two bureaucrats arrived and started asking questions so that, like they said, he could be "processed." It was funny! Like when they were asking for his address, Jim Grossi said, "Heaven," and Lupita Carrion said there was no zip code there.

And Horton, when they asked God when he was born, said, "Just before 1 B.C. Actually, that's not right, is it?" He turned to me and asked, "Do you know when God was born?" This made me feel very good, because Horton never asks anybody anything. He just naturally knows all the answers. I said that God was there always, and you couldn't put a date on that.

One of the social workers was on the phone all this time, and within an hour she got God pegged as "one José Martinez." They had a file on him. It seems that a lot of social workers, on and off, were trying to get him out of his parents' house and into a foster home.

I asked about that, whether they were doing it out of love or fear that he might be killed. And they told me it was their job to protect children they believed to be abused.

"You sure didn't do your job, because José Martinez died last Friday." That's what I told them.

"You people," Horton was shouting, "are paid to protect little kids. What I want to know is how many times he got beat up and why didn't you take

him away from his parents?"

They were very cool and polite and said that because José Martinez couldn't talk, he was considered a handicapped child and it wasn't easy to place him in a foster home.

After they said that, Horton just told them off.

"It's never going to happen again," he said. "I'm going to organize people, and we're going to really start protecting little kids. We're going to be all over the place, watching over them. You just wait and see. Things are going to change. If it takes me all my life, that's what I'm going to do, protect little kids. And there will be millions of us, watching over them so they won't get hurt any more."

It was wonderful to see how determined he was and how the others felt about it too. They were so busy organizing themselves that they didn't notice that God was being taken away. But I noticed that his body was all covered with hurts, just like when I first saw him.

I followed the grown-ups to the car and said that I had to go with José. I said "José" instead of "God" so they wouldn't give me any problems. And they said I could go, because they were going to take him home and ask about how he got the bruises and all.

The Martinezes lived in the building right next to Mr. Skarbinski's empty lot, and as we pulled up to the building I asked if I could have some time with the kid alone, and the welfare people said it was all right, because they would go up and see his parents, and we could wait in the car.

It was so hard to look at him, with all his bruises, and I was crying anyway, so I closed my eyes. And that's when God spoke to me. He said that they had buried José's body in the empty lot at night. And I looked over at the lot, and right in front of my eyes it happened! Flowers were growing all over it! It was the most beautiful thing I've ever seen, and I turned to tell God that it was a great miracle he was performing, but he wasn't there. He just wasn't there any more.

"Oh, God, don't leave me!" I shouted then, because I was so scared that he was gone and I wouldn't ever see him again. And it was then that I heard my voice.

"Christian, I will be with you always," the voice said.